# GROWN-UP GABBY

by TONY GARTH

More than anything else, Gabby wanted to be grown up. She wore her mother's hats and high-heeled shoes and borrowed her big sister's make-up.

Being a little girl was boring.

"Are you coming out to play?" her friends asked. "It'll be fun. We're pretending to be pixies and elves today."

But Gabby was much too grown up for silly pretending games.

"Sorry," she said. "I'm having my hair done."

"Look what I've got for you," said Gabby's Dad, when he came home from work. "A Mandy Mop Top Doll! You can comb her hair and she talks when you press her tummy!"

"Oh really, Dad," sighed Gabby. "I'm much too old for dolls. Couldn't I have a new lipstick instead?"

Gabby's Mum and Dad looked at each other and shook their heads in dismay.

At bedtime, Gabby insisted on putting on her own nightie and brushing her own teeth. Just like a grown up.

"Would you like me to read you a bedtime story?" asked her Mum.

"Oh really, Mum," Gabby sighed again. "I'm much too old for bedtime stories."

"So you won't be needing George then," said her Mum, pointing to Gabby's old teddy bear.

"George isn't a toy," insisted Gabby. "He more like a...a...sort of mascot. Just leave him on the table."

"All right," said her Mum. "Goodnight, then."

As soon as her Mum had closed the door, Gabby picked up George and gave him a big hug. Then she fell asleep.

Next morning, Gabby woke up bright and early. She turned over to say "Good Morning" to George. But George was nowhere to be seen!

Gabby looked in her cupboard and under her bed. In fact, she looked everywhere. But there was just no sign of George.

Gabby began to feel very upset. She loved her old teddy bear more than anything. But she didn't want anyone thinking that she wasn't grown up after all.

She ran downstairs.

"Mum! Mum," she cried. "George has gone! I can't find him anywhere!"

"Perhaps he thought you didn't need him anymore now you're so grown up," her Mum suggested.

Gabby's eyes began to fill with tears.

"Don't worry," said her Mum. "I'll help you look for him."

Gabby ran off to find her Dad.

"Dad! Dad!" she wailed. "George has vanished!"

"I thought you were much too old for teddy bears," her Dad said.

Gabby burst into tears...

"I AM NOT GROWN UP!" she sobbed. "AND I WANT MY TEDDY BACK!"

Gabby's Mum and Dad searched high and low for George. Eventually, they found him...tucked away in Rex's dog basket!

"Rex must have taken him from your room last night," said Gabby's Dad. He picked George up and handed him back to Gabby.

Gabby hugged George as hard as she could.

"I promise I'll never be grown up again," she told him.

George wasn't the only one who looked relieved. So did Gabby's parents. "That's nice, dear," said her Mum.

"After all," said Gabby, "Everyone should have a lucky mascot, shouldn't they?"

# Look out for the next six Little Monsters!

HELPFUL HENRY

SHY SOPHIE

BOSSY BETHANY

REVOLTING RONNIE

WORRIED WINNIE

TV TREVOR